Acknowledgments: Cover, endpapers and title page illustrations by James Hodgson. Photograph on page 10 by Seaphot.

The Ladybird Book of DRAGONS

The Magic Vase

written and illustrated by Peter Longden

Long ago in a far off land there lived a woodcutter and his son. Their home was a humble cottage by the edge of a great forest.

The woodcutter worked hard and long for a little money, but though he was poor he was content.

The woodcutter's son Edgar didn't share his father's love of the forest life, and he longed for better things.

One day young Edgar was out wandering when something caught his eye. It was a large vase half hidden in the undergrowth. Carefully Edgar freed the vase from its resting place, rubbing it with his sleeve to remove the grime.

As he rubbed, the vase seemed to shudder and shake in his hands. Then to Edgar's amazement, out popped a huge dragon.

'How did you get in there?' gasped Edgar.

'It's a magic vase,' replied the dragon, 'and I'm a Genie, a *magic* Genie, a magic *dragon* Genie!'

'I'm dreaming, I must be,' stammered Edgar.

'It's no dream,' laughed the dragon. 'When you rubbed the vase, I was freed to come to you.'

Edgar sat down in the grass, staring up wonderingly.

'My name is Gilbert,' the dragon went on, 'and I've been cooped up in that vase for the past hundred years. As a matter of fact, you're the very first person to summon me.'

2

4

'What do you want?' asked Edgar, nervously.

'I want to help you,' replied Gilbert. 'I'm allowed to grant you three wishes, and you may ask for anything in the world.'

Edgar thought for a while; he could hardly believe his luck. 'I hate it here in the woods,' he said at last. 'There's no fun at all. I wish I could swop places with the happiest person in the country.'

The dragon raised his front paws above his head and said, 'So let it be.'

In an instant Edgar was shivering high up on a mountain top, surrounded by hundreds of sheep.

'What on earth am I doing here?' thought the boy. 'Whose are these sheep and why am I dressed in these silly clothes? — Where's that dragon?' Gilbert suddenly appeared, laughing loudly.

'I'm dressed in worse rags than I wore before!' said Edgar, crossly. 'And why am I stuck up here on this lonely mountain?'

'You are now the happiest man in the country,' replied Gilbert, 'and the happiest man just happens to be a shepherd, a really happy shepherd!'

'But I seem to be even poorer than before,' said Edgar. 'I wish I was the richest man in the country instead.'

Once again Gilbert raised his paws, and the foolish boy found himself in a huge castle surrounded by wealth.

Edgar was strolling around his new home, extremely pleased with his new found fortune, when he caught sight of himself in a mirror.

'I'm old!' he roared. 'An old man; a *very* old man,' and then he thought, 'Ah well, at least I'm an extremely *rich* old man,' and he grinned and strutted off.

As the days passed Edgar discovered that the life of the richest man in the country was not quite what he'd expected. He didn't even have as much fun as he'd had in the forest.

'This won't do at all,' he said to himself, and once again he summoned the dragon.

'Yes, master?' said Gilbert, popping his head through an open window.

'I'm not at all happy as the richest man in the country,' said Edgar. 'All I do is count my gold coins day after day — it's boring! I'm nothing but a miser, and a miserable one at that!'

'Then make your final wish,' laughed Gilbert.

'You and your wishes,' said Edgar, sadly. 'I'll tell you one thing I wish — I wish I'd never found that old vase in the first place!'

No sooner had he spoken than Edgar found himself back in the forest.

'I feel strange,' said Edgar, 'very strange indeed.' And as he headed home, he began to realise just how lucky he was to be the son of a fine and happy woodcutter.

Perhaps it was true, as his father often said, the simplest things in life were often the best.

5

The Dragon who was Kind

by Hugh Pearson-Gee
illustrated by Mark Astel

One thousand years ago, one day
A wizard laid a spell
Upon a baby dragon who
Had drunk from out his well.

This spell he laid upon the beast –
The worst that he could find –
To sleep throughout a thousand years
And then to wake up KIND!

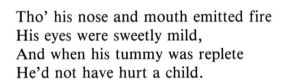

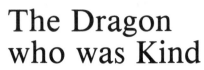

Tho' his nose and mouth emitted fire
His eyes were sweetly mild,
And when his tummy was replete
He'd not have hurt a child.

The dragon was the 'spiky' sort
And surely you'd have said
"Not quite the kind of beast that I
Would like to take to bed!"

He wore his spikes all down his back,
With spikes his head was crowned;
His fiery breath had burnt the grass
For several yards around!

And while he slept an earthquake had
Encased him in a grave,
So when he woke and wriggled out
He left behind a cave.

A great galumphing brute he was,
With bony paws that sank
Into the earth and made a mess
Like a great big army tank.

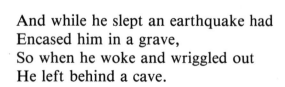

6

Now, when he woke he'd not had food
For quite a thousand years!
The very thought will fill your eyes
With sympathetic tears.

So down the hillside he did go
With speed you'd ne'er believe,
And tried to find some living meat
His hunger to relieve.

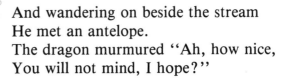

His thirst he first did seek to quench
And hurried to a stream,
But when he took a second gulp
He heard the fishes scream.

"Oh! Mr Dragon, please do stop.
You'll drown us in the air!"
"I'll die of thirst," the dragon said,
"But I really must be fair.

"So if you want this river I
Will wander on and see
If I can find one large enough
For fishes and for me."

And wandering on beside the stream
He met an antelope.
The dragon murmured "Ah, how nice,
You will not mind, I hope?"

Whether he did or did not care
Our dragon could not say,
The antelope was terrified;
It could not run away.

The dragon hooked him on a claw,
To chew him at his ease
When up came Mrs Antelope
And fell upon her knees.

She begged and wept and wept and begged,
"Please set my husband free!"
And hungry though the dragon was
He sadly did agree.

7

For down at root our dragon was
A gentleman, you see.
When talking to a lady
One's mouth should empty be.

So out he pulled the antelope
And set him on his feet.
He thanked the dragon very much
And beat a quick retreat.

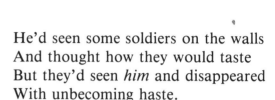

He'd seen some soldiers on the walls
And thought how they would taste
But they'd seen *him* and disappeared
With unbecoming haste.

They dropped the "port" and raised the
"bridge"
And ran away to hide.
He slithered up the wall and down
And found himself inside.

Soon afterwards he met a goat
Who, when he tried to eat it
Just turned his head and crossly said,
"My lad, you'd better beat it!"

And other things he tried to eat
Made such polite excuses
Our poor KIND dragon just supposed
They had some other uses.

One day he drew near to a town,
He chortled loud with glee
And when a dragon "chortles", it
Sounds louder than the sea.

He gazed around and saw a house
And knocked upon the door
Whereon the house fell in, and pinned
Its owners to the floor.

The dragon was the most upset
Because the house fell down,
He helped the people from the wreck
And hurried out of town.

The dragon felt quite tired of life
And up a hill did wander
And met a hermit who did pray
And think and sigh and ponder.

"Good day, fair sir," the hermit said,
"I scarce know how to greet you."
The dragon gasped, "Oh, mister man,
Oh, please, please, may I eat you?"

"I'd rather not, if you don't mind,
And be careful where you tread.
I've sowed some lettuce seeds this spring
To have some with my bread.

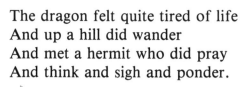

"I'm sure you'd like to have some too,
They're very good to eat."
"Oh no," the starving dragon cried,
"I only live on meat."

The dragon and the hermit talked
of "why" and "how" and "what"
And, quite between ourselves, they talked
An awful lot of rot.

By morning they'd decided
That they should fly away
To seek their food and fortune,
And a better place to stay.

The dragon sprang up in the air
The hermit on his back.
The hermit only wore a skin
So he didn't have to pack.

They flew together on and on
To the rising of the sun.
The dragon thought it hungry work;
The hermit thought it fun.

9

One day just as the sun had set,
They were flying over China.
They saw a palace wrapped in flame –
There could be no sight finer.

The dragon swept to earth at once
Dropped through the smoky haze
And as he flew, the wind he made
Blew out the fearful blaze.

The dragon found himself a cave
Beneath the city walls,
And all the Chinese children loved
To go and pay him calls.

He had his food provided free
And always served the Crown.
He worked for it and fought for it
And won it great renown.

The Emperor called the hermit in
And thanked him most benignly,
And had the dear old dragon fed
In Chinese fashion, finely.

Then in return the hermit was
Rewarded with a wife,
And told to stay and live at Court
For all his natural life.

His simple nature made him loved
(He never used to brag),
And though he's dead this thousand years
He lives upon their flag.

The Komodo Dragon

by John Paull

Years ago, English sailors on round the world trips sometimes called at the group of islands called Indonesia to collect fresh food and water. When they returned to England, they talked about all the amazing wildlife they had seen on the tropical islands — fruit-eating bats, tigers, elephants, orang-utans — and even dragons!

Few people believed these tales, but in 1912, an expedition went to Indonesia to find out the truth — and found a creature that really *did* look like a dragon. It had flashing teeth, a long whip-lash tail, and a scaly body.

The explorers called it a Komodo Dragon, after the island where it was found, but it wasn't a dragon at all. It was a member of the family of lizards called Monitors. It was three metres long, and weighed about one hundred and fifty kilograms.

It is believed that the Komodo Dragon is a descendant of giant reptiles long extinct, and probably related to a creature which lived millions of years ago in Australia. These rare lizards are now a protected species, and no one is allowed to kill or capture them as they roam in the hot forests of the Indonesian islands.

The Dale Dragon

by Wynter Weston
illustrated by Frank Humphris

When the weather was good, the Bradley family often went for a walk in the Derbyshire dales. Today the children had gone on ahead, because the grown-ups had stopped for a rest. Brendan and Serina had never been in this particular dale before. There was a steep rock face on one side and they pretended they were mountaineers. The bottom of the dale was overgrown with bushes and nettles, and quite large pieces of rock were strewn on the path where they were now walking in single file.

Brendan looked back and called to his sister, 'Hurry up, there's a cave up here.'

She was just about to ask where, when she heard a strange voice, deep and hollow. She thought at first that Brendan was playing some game, but then she saw he was standing stock still, listening, just as she was.

The voice grunted again, 'Oh dear! Ouch! I'll never get out — Ow!'

'I think it's coming from the cave over there,' said Brendan. 'Let's just creep a bit closer and find out what it is.'

'Oh no! Let's go back — I'm frightened,' said Serina.

'It's all right, we'll be careful. If we creep up behind those bushes, we can see the cave, without being seen ourselves,' said Brendan as he crept forward stealthily. Serina followed him, too scared to remain alone.

They heard more puffing and grunting as they crouched down behind the bushes. Serina could see the cave now, through the plants growing near the entrance, and it wasn't very big. The puffing grew louder, then they heard the deep hollow voice again. 'Oh dear! I wish I hadn't come in here. I'll never get out. Oh my goodness me!' Suddenly there was a deep cough, and a large puff of smoke came out of the cave!

This was enough for Brendan. 'Come on,' he said. 'Let's get out of here.'

As Serina turned, she tripped and kicked a pebble. As it bounced along the ground, there was a surprised silence from the cave. Then the voice said, 'Please don't run away. I won't hurt you, I promise. I'm not fierce or cruel. Everybody always thinks that dragons are always fierce and hungry — so I never have any friends. I'm very lonely.'

He licked his big red nostrils with an equally big red tongue and wisps of smoke, still hanging round them, disappeared. Then he spoke again. 'My name is Stride,' he boomed. 'I live in this dale and you are the first humans who have ever been kind enough to stop when I called to them!'

The voice went on, 'I'll just clear these bushes away and then we can see each other. Don't you think that's a good idea? Wait a minute — don't be afraid, I won't hurt you.'

Suddenly a great sheet of flame leaped through the high grass and bushes between the children and the cave. There was a loud crackling and hissing as the dry material disappeared in flames. The children were much too frightened to speak or move. The flames died down, and as the wisps of grey-blue smoke cleared, they saw him!

He was about half-way out of the cave. His head was almost as big as an elephant's, but it was shaped rather like a horse's. His eyes were black and his nostrils big and red. He seemed to squat over his front legs, which were strong and short, and great yellow claws showed from the ends of them. He was a deep green colour, striped like a tiger with bright orange stripes. He looked very strong, very fierce and very handsome.

The children stayed still, hardly breathing. Then Brendan managed to stammer, 'We're a bit frightened!'

13

'Oh, please don't be frightened!' said the dragon. 'I'm not going to hurt you, you know. It's just that I'm so big and ugly – that's what makes you scared.' He went on, 'I want to talk, that's all. I'm so lonely. I never have anyone to talk to, because everything is so frightened of me.'

The dragon shifted his great legs slightly and sniffed unhappily. This made the children stiffen, but they were beginning to realise that the dragon meant them no harm.

'What do you like to eat?' asked Brendan, rather anxiously.

'Curiously enough,' replied the dragon, 'I have a very small appetite. I eat grass and berries when I can get them. In fact I like all fruit, but it means leaving the dale to get it, and I can only do that at night, because I might be seen.'

Serina, who had not yet spoken, whispered, 'You're out today and *we've* seen you.

'Ah well, that's different,' he said. 'This cave is rather small and I don't usually stay here. I got cramp so badly, I came out to stretch myself, and then of course I saw you two.'

Serina grew a little bolder. 'I don't think you're ugly at all!' she said. 'I think you're nice.'

'How kind you are,' said Stride. 'I'm so pleased I saw you. What are you doing in the dale?'

Brendan explained. 'We're out for the afternoon with our parents. They've stopped for a rest.'

Stride yawned. 'Excuse me. I'm tired. I didn't sleep very well yesterday. So, you're with your parents.'

'Didn't you sleep last night?' asked Serina.

The dragon closed his eyes.

'Oh no, I never sleep at night you know. I have to go out at night and sleep during the day. I have to arrange my life like that.'

By now the children were growing braver and moved nearer to Stride, in order to get a closer look at him. Almost immediately they heard voices, and Stride quickly got to his feet, making the children jump back in alarm. 'Is that your parents?' he asked.

'No,' said Brendan, 'it's someone coming down from that end,' and he pointed up the dale, where by now, a number of people were coming into sight.

The children could see that it was a party of walkers moving towards them. They had packs on their backs.

Serina turned to Stride to ask him about what he was going to do, and found he'd disappeared. As she turned back to Brendan, the first walker came up.

'Hello!' he said. 'Isn't it hot! Have you any idea how far it is to the footbridge over the river?'

'Well, it's quite a long walk,' said Brendan. 'I don't know exactly how far. I'm not very good at judging distances.'

'That's all right,' laughed the hiker. 'Just as long as we're heading in the right direction!'

The rest of the party reached the children, greeting them cheerfully and passing on. As the children watched them go, they heard one say, 'I'm sure I could smell smoke a few minutes ago.'

There was a hollow cough behind them, and they turned quickly to see Stride stretching his legs out contentedly, as he lay in the hot sunshine.

'How did you do that?' asked Serina.

'How did I do what?' said Stride.

'Disappear like that as soon as those people appeared?

Stride snorted and wisps of smoke curled from his nostrils. 'Disappear? Not me!' he said.

'Those people didn't see you,' said Brendan.

The dragon sniffed. 'They're grown-ups, aren't they? They wouldn't see a dragon, because they don't believe in them.'

15

He scratched his nose with a giant claw and added, 'Grown-ups can't see anything they don't believe in.'

'I didn't know that,' said Serina, 'but we couldn't see you either.'

'That's right, we couldn't,' said Brendan, sitting down on a large piece of rock.

'That's because you were thinking about those people,' replied Stride. 'That's what happens when you're not concentrating.'

'Mum's always telling Brendan that he doesn't concentrate enough!' laughed Serina.

'Shut up,' grumbled Brendan. 'Just wait and see what she says to you when you tell her you've seen a dragon.'

Before Serina could reply, Stride said, 'I shouldn't bother if I were you.'

'Do you mean, don't tell Mum?' said Serina.

The dragon moved into a more comfortable position.

'I mean, don't tell *anyone*,' he said. 'They'll only say, "What imaginations you children have!" You might as well keep it to yourself.'

'That's a pity,' said Brendan. 'It's not everyone who's met a dragon! It would be great to tell my friends.'

'Please yourself!' said Stride. 'But don't say I didn't tell you what to expect!'

Serina settled down on a rock beside her brother. The sun shone and insects winged from flower to flower on the dale side.

'Stride's right, Brendan,' she said. 'Everyone would make fun of us. It's our secret – it's lovely and I'm not going to tell anyone else.'

She looked over at Stride, who seemed to be dozing.

'I think you're a very handsome dragon,' she said. Her voice sounded very sleepy. She may not even have heard Stride's reply.

'Thank you, dear!' he said. 'You're very kind.'

* * * * * *

The grown-ups were very warm and a bit irritable as they hurried to catch up with the children.

'Just look at that!' said Dad, who was in the lead. Mum came up and looked over his shoulder along the narrow path. The two children were half lying, half sitting, among some boulders. They were very still and Mum said, 'They look as if they're asleep.'

Their voices roused the dozing children.

'Hello, you two. Wake up and we'll go and have a cup of tea,' said Mum.

Then Dad saw the charred bushes. 'Look at that!' he said, 'some careless fellow has been throwing cigarette ends down. They should have more sense, this dry weather — everything's as dry as tinder.'

Brendan and Serina smiled knowingly at each other as they stood up and followed their parents.

The party moved on up the path. The dale widened into a grassy paddock and the rock sides became much less steep. The silent children saw the top of a bus over the stone wall in the distance. 'There's the road,' Dad said. 'I can see our car now.'

As the four reached a gate in the wall, Serina tugged at her brother's shirt.

'Look!' she whispered. 'Look at that!' He looked up and saw a wooden signpost with three words on it — FOOTPATH TO STRIDESDALE. Serina stood for a moment and looked back along the dale. 'Magic,' she said.

17

The Dragon's Thorn

by Mary Hurt

illustrated by Brian Price Thomas

Many years ago in an eastern land, there lived a crafty dragon whose den was in a forest. This forest was a very pleasant place and many people enjoyed strolling through it. The dragon liked to sit in his den and wait until he could hear footsteps approaching. Then he would lie down and start to make loud moaning noises as if he was in great pain.

'Oh, help! Somebody help me!' he would groan. 'There's a thorn stuck in my foot. Please come and help me to pull it out.'

The kindhearted passer-by would enter the den to help, and the dragon would then pounce upon him and gobble him up. (For he did not have a thorn in his foot at all.) He was a sly old dragon, wasn't he? And because no one had ever escaped from him to tell the tale of his awful trick, people continued to walk in the forest and get caught.

One day a clever young man passed by the dragon's den, and the dragon started moaning and groaning once again.

'Oh, help me! Somebody help! Won't somebody please pull this thorn out of my foot?' he called.

Now the young man was clever indeed. Instead of going straight inside to help, he stood a little way back from the entrance and had a good look at the ground nearby. There he noticed something very mysterious.

'Tell me,' he said, 'why is it that there are lots of different footprints leading into your den and only your own coming out?'

The dragon was so surprised at this question that he stopped moaning, and tried to think of a good excuse to answer the question. But while he was thinking, it did not take the young man very long to work out for himself that people who entered the dragon's den did not come out again – because they had been eaten up! At once he rushed away, terrified that he too would be gobbled up, and he ran all the way to the emperor's palace and told him what he had discovered.

The emperor was very interested to hear this and thanked the young man enormously. Then he sent his messengers far and wide to warn all the people in the land of the dragon's terrible secret. So for a long time no one ever walked in that forest.

Some years passed, and the story was gradually forgotten. People did not warn their children any more. So one day a boy called Ying Wong, who had never heard of the dragon, rode his horse through the forest. As he passed close by the dragon's den, he was most surprised to hear loud moaning noises. Riding on slowly, he came upon the dragon rolling around and groaning, obviously in great pain.

'Oh, help me! Won't somebody help? There's a thorn in my foot, and I can hardly bear the pain.'

No one had ever told Ying Wong about the dragon's trick, and he was a very kind and helpful boy who could not bear to see a creature in pain. He went up to the dragon and gently lifted up its paw. And do you know, there really was a huge sharp thorn sticking into the dragon's foot!

He removed the thorn carefully, and bathed the foot with water from a nearby stream. Then pulling off his shirt, he tore it into strips and with these he bandaged the dragon's foot.

The dragon was very pleased, because his foot didn't hurt any more. He thanked Ying Wong, saying, 'I will never forget your kindness. One day I hope I will be able to repay you.'

So, saying goodbye, the boy rode away and continued on his journey.

Later, when he became a young man, Ying Wong fell in love with the Emperor's daughter and married her. When her father died some time afterwards, Ying Wong became Emperor in his place. He was kind and good, and the people loved him dearly, living very peacefully under his rule for many years.

Then the Emperor of a nearby country decided that he would send his army to attack the country of Ying Wong. The enemy soldiers were strong and fierce, and numbered many thousands. Ying Wong's army had lived in peace for so long that his soldiers were not used to fighting. They could not possibly beat the attacking army.

Ying Wong was very worried, and wondered what to do. Then he remembered his friend, the dragon, and the promise that the dragon had made to him.

Quickly he set off on his horse for the dragon's den in the forest, and he found him snoozing in a sunny spot.

'Hello!' he said, standing a little way away. 'Do you remember me? I pulled out a thorn from your foot many years ago.'

The dragon looked up in great surprise. 'Of course I remember,' he replied, with delight. 'How could I forget? You are the only person who has ever been kind to me.'

'Well,' Ying Wong went on, 'the time has come at last for you to help me in return. The country is in great trouble.' And he told the dragon how he had become the Emperor, and about the army which was about to attack.

The dragon was very glad he could help his friend. He went home with Ying Wong to the palace, and together they made a plan.

When the enemy army attacked, Ying Wong's soldiers were led into battle by the dragon, who was an enormous and terrifying beast, as you can imagine. His black scaly body gleamed from head to toe, and his horny claws scratched furiously at the ground beneath him. His long glistening tail flicked from side to side above him, and the fire that shot from his mouth was terrifying indeed. The strong fierce soldiers took one look, and turned and fled. They were never seen again.

From that day on, the country of Ying Wong was left in peace. The dragon came to live in the gardens of the palace, and he became everybody's friend. No longer did people go in fear of him, and he protected the country for many years afterwards.

The Last of the Dragons

by E. Nesbit

illustrated by Joy Shufflebotham

Of course you know that dragons were once as common as buses are now, and almost as dangerous. But as every well-brought-up prince was expected to kill a dragon, and rescue a princess, the dragons grew fewer and fewer, till it was often quite hard for a princess to find a dragon to be rescued from. And at last there were no more dragons in France and no more dragons in Germany, or Spain, or Italy, or Russia. There were some left in China, and are still, but they are cold and bronzy, and there were never any, of course, in America. But the last real live dragon left was in England, and of course that was a very long time ago, before what you call English History began.

This dragon lived in Cornwall in the big caves amidst the rocks, and a very fine big dragon it was, quite seventy feet long from the tip of its fearful snout to the end of its terrible tail. It breathed fire and smoke, and rattled when it walked, because its scales were made of iron. Its wings were like half-umbrellas — or like bat's wings, only several thousand times bigger. Everyone was very frightened of it, and well they might be.

Now the King of Cornwall had one daughter, and when she was sixteen, she would have to go and face the dragon. Such tales are always told in royal nurseries at bedtime, so the princess knew what she had to expect. The dragon would not eat her, of course, because a prince would come and rescue her. But the princess could not help thinking it would be much pleasanter to have nothing to do with the dragon at all — not even to be rescued from him.

'All the princes I know are such very silly little boys,' she told her father. 'Why must I be rescued by a prince?'

'It's always done, my dear,' said the king, taking his crown off and putting it on the grass, for they were alone in the garden, and even kings must unbend sometimes.

'Father, darling,' said the princess presently, when she had made a daisy chain and put it on the king's head, where the crown ought to have been. 'Father, darling, couldn't we tie up one of the silly little princes for the dragon to look at — and then I could go and kill the dragon and rescue the prince? I fence much better than any of the princes we know.'

'What an unladylike idea!' said the king, and put his crown on again, for he saw the prime minister coming. 'Dismiss the thought, my child. I rescued your mother from a dragon, and you don't want to set yourself up above her, I should hope?'

'But this is the *last* dragon. It is different from all other dragons.'

'How?' asked the king.

'Because he *is* the last,' said the princess, and went off to her fencing lessons, with which she took great pains. She took great pains with all her lessons — for she could not give up the idea of fighting the dragon. She took such pains that she became the strongest and boldest and most skilful and most sensible princess in Europe. She had always been the prettiest and nicest.

And the days and years went on, till at last the day came which was the day before the princess was to be rescued from the dragon. The prince who was to do this deed of valour was a pale prince, with large eyes and a head full of mathematics and philosophy, but he had unfortunately neglected his fencing lessons. He was to stay the night at the palace, and there was a banquet.

After supper the princess sent her pet parrot to the prince with a note. It said: 'Please, Prince, come on to the terrace. I want to talk to you without anybody else hearing. — The Princess.'

So, of course, he went — and he saw her gown of silver a long way off shining among the shadows of the trees like water in starlight. And when he came quite close to her he said: 'Princess, at your service,' and bent his cloth-of-gold-covered knee and put his hand on his cloth-of-gold-covered heart.

'Do you think,' said the princess earnestly, 'that you will be able to kill the dragon?'

'I will kill the dragon,' said the prince firmly, 'or perish in the attempt.'

'It's no use your perishing,' said the princess.

'It's the least I can do,' said the prince.

'What I'm afraid of is that it'll be the most you can do,' said the princess.

'It's the only thing I can do,' said he, 'unless I kill the dragon.'

'Why you should do *anything* for me is what I can't see,' said she.

'But I want to,' he said. 'You must know that I love you better than anything in the world.'

When he said that he looked so kind that the princess began to like him a little.

'Look here,' she said, 'no one else will go out tomorrow. You know they tie me to a rock, and leave me — and then everybody scurries home and puts up the shutters and keeps them shut till you ride through the town in triumph shouting that you've killed the dragon, and I ride on the horse behind you weeping for joy.'

'I've heard that that is how it is done,' said he.

'Well, do you love me well enough to come very quickly and set me free — and we'll fight the dragon together?'

'It wouldn't be safe for you.'

'Much safer for both of us for me to be free, with a sword in my hand, than tied up and helpless. *Do* agree.'

He could refuse her nothing. So he agreed. And next day everything happened as she had said.

When he had cut the cords that tied her to the rocks, they stood on the lonely mountain-side looking at each other.

'It seems to me,' said the prince, 'that this ceremony could have been arranged without the dragon.'

'Yes,' said the princess, 'but since it has been arranged *with* the dragon —'

'It seems such a pity to kill the dragon — the last in the world,' said the prince.

23

'Well, then, don't let's,' said the princess. 'Let's tame it and teach it not to eat princesses but to eat out of their hands. They say everything can be tamed by kindness.'

'Taming by kindness means giving them things to eat,' said the prince. 'Have you got anything to eat?'

She hadn't, but it turned out that the prince had a few biscuits. 'Breakfast was so very early,' said he, 'and I thought you might have felt faint after the fight.'

'How clever,' said the princess, and they took a biscuit in each hand. And they looked here and they looked there, but never a dragon could they see.

'But here's its trail,' said the prince, and pointed to where the rock was scarred and scratched, making a track which led to the mouth of a dark cave. It was like cart-ruts in a farm road, mixed with the marks of sea-gulls' feet on the sea-sand. 'Look, that's where it's dragged its brass tail and planted its steel claws.'

'Don't let's think how hard its tail and its claws are,' said the princess, 'or I shall begin to be frightened – and I know you can't tame anything, even by kindness, if you're frightened of it. Come on. Now or never.'

She caught the prince's hand in hers and they ran along the path towards the dark mouth of the cave. But they did not run into it. It really was so very *dark*.

So they stood outside, and the prince shouted: 'What ho! Dragon there! What ho within!' And from the cave they heard an answering voice and great clattering and creaking. It sounded as though a rather large cotton-mill were stretching itself and waking up out of its sleep.

The prince and the princess trembled, but they stood firm.

'Dragon – I say, Dragon!' said the princess, 'do come out and talk to us. We've brought you a present.'

'Oh, yes – I know your presents,' growled the dragon in a huge rumbling voice, 'One of those precious princesses, I suppose? And I've got to come out and fight for her. Well, I tell you straight, I'm not going to do it. A fair fight I wouldn't say no to – a fair fight and no favour – but one of these put-up fights where you've got to lose – No. If I wanted a princess I'd come and take her, in my own time – but I don't. What do you suppose I'd do with her, if I'd got her?'

24

'Eat her, wouldn't you?' said the princess in a voice that trembled a little.

'Eat nothing!' said the dragon very rudely. 'I wouldn't touch the horrid thing.'

The princess's voice grew firmer.

'Do you like biscuits?' she asked.

'*No*,' growled the dragon.

'Not the nice little expensive ones with sugar on the top?'

'No,' growled the dragon.

'Then what *do* you like?' asked the prince.

'You go away and don't bother me,' growled the dragon, and they could hear it turn over with a great clanging and clattering.

The prince and princess looked at each other. What *were* they to do? Of course it was no use going home and telling the king that the dragon didn't want princesses – because His Majesty was very old-fashioned and would never have believed that a new-fashioned dragon could ever be at all different from an old-fashioned dragon. They could not go into the cave and kill the dragon. Indeed, unless he attacked the princess it did not seem fair to kill him at all.

'He must like something,' whispered the princess, and she called out in a voice as sweet as honey and sugar-cane: 'Dragon – Dragon dear!'

'WHAT?' shouted the dragon. 'Say that again!' and they could hear the dragon coming towards them through the darkness of the cave. The princess shivered, and said in a very small voice: 'Dragon – Dragon dear!'

And then the dragon came out. The prince drew his sword, and the princess drew hers – the beautiful silver-handled one that the prince had brought in his motor-car. But they did not attack; they moved slowly back as the dragon came out, all the vast scaly length of him, and lay along the rock – his great wings half-spread and his silvery sheen gleaming like diamonds in the sun. At last they could retreat no further – the dark rock behind them stopped their way – and with their backs to the rock they stood swords in hand and waited.

The dragon drew nearer and nearer – and now they could see that he was not breathing fire and smoke as they had expected – he came crawling slowly towards them wriggling a little as a puppy does when it wants to play and isn't quite sure whether you're not cross with it.

'Your kindness quite undragons me,' it said. 'No one has ever asked any of us what we like to eat — always offering us princesses, and then rescuing them — and never once, ''What'll you take to drink the king's health in?'' Cruel hard I call it.' and it wept again.

'But what would you like to drink our health in?' said the prince. 'We're going to be married today, aren't we, Princess?'

She said that she supposed so.

'What'll I take to drink your health in?' asked the dragon. 'Ah, you're something like a gentleman, you are, sir. I don't mind if I do, sir. I'll be proud to drink you and your good lady's health in a little drop of' — its voice faltered — 'to think of you asking me so friendly like,' it said. 'Yes, sir, just a little drop of petrol that's what does a dragon good, sir —'

'I've lots in the car,' said the prince, and was off down the mountain like a flash. He was a good judge of character, and he knew that with *this* dragon the princess would be safe.

'If I might make so bold,' said the dragon, 'while the gentleman's away — p'raps just to pass the time you'd be so kind as to call me Dear again, and if you'd shake claws with a poor old dragon that's never been anybody's enemy but his own — well, the last of the dragons'll be the proudest dragon there's ever been since the first of them.'

And then they saw that great tears were coursing down its brazen cheek.

'Whatever's the matter?' said the prince.

'Nobody,' sobbed the dragon, 'ever called me ''dear'' before!'

'Don't cry, dragon dear,' said the princess. 'We'll call you ''dear'' as often as you like. We want to tame you.'

'I *am* tame,' said the dragon — 'that's just it. That's what nobody but you has ever found out. I'm so tame that I'd eat out of your hands.'

'Eat what, dragon dear?' said the princess. 'Not biscuits?'

The dragon slowly shook its heavy head.

'Not biscuits?' said the princess tenderly. 'What, then, dragon dear?'

It held out an enormous paw, and the great steel hooks that were its claws closed softly and gently over the princess's hand.

And so the prince and princess went back to the palace in triumph, the dragon following them like a pet dog. And all through the wedding festivities no one drank more earnestly to the happiness of the bride and bridegroom than the princess's pet dragon — whom she had at once named Fido.

And when the happy pair were settled in their own kingdom, Fido came to them and begged to be allowed to make himself useful.

'There must be some little thing I can do,' he said, rattling his wings and stretching his claws. 'My wings and claws and so on ought to be turned to some account — to say nothing of my grateful heart.'

So the prince had a special saddle or howdah made for him — very long it was — like the tops of many buses fitted together. One hundred and fifty seats were fitted to this, and the dragon, whose greatest pleasure was now to give pleasure to others, delighted in taking parties of children to the seaside. It flew through the air quite easily with its hundred and fifty little passengers — and would lie on the sand patiently waiting till they were ready to return. The children were very fond of it and used to call it Dear, a word which never failed to bring tears of affection and gratitude to its eyes. So it lived, useful and respected, till quite the other day — when some one happened to say, in his hearing, that dragons were out of date, now that so much new machinery had come in. This so distressed him that he asked the king to change him into something less old-fashioned, and the kindly monarch at once changed him into a mechanical contrivance. The dragon, indeed, became the first aeroplane.

Fabulous Chinese Dragons

written and illustrated by Ron Jackson

In old China, it was believed that there were several sorts of dragons.

The most powerful was the *Lung*. It was the symbol of the Chinese emperors, and was thought to have

> the head of a camel
> the horns of a deer
> the eyes of a rabbit
> the ears of a crow
> the neck of a snake
> the belly of a frog
> the scales of a fish
> the claws of a hawk, and
> the palm of a tiger!

It had wings, and lived in the sky.

The *Le* lived in the ocean, and the *Keaou* lived in marshes and in caves in the mountains.

These three dragons were very important and had great power over people's lives.

Dragons in all countries are connected with storms and rivers and mists. In ancient times it was believed that if they were angry, they could stop the rains and flowing rivers. So people used to make gifts and offerings to the dragons, to make sure that there was plenty of rain and a good supply of water.

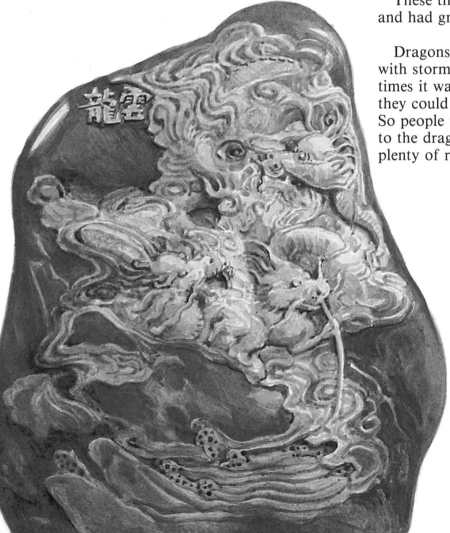

A small eighteenth-century soapstone carving showing a dragon in the clouds

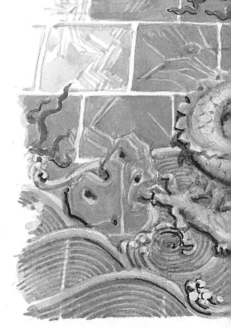

28

Wood engraving

This was particularly important in China, because of the rice growing. Since dragons were so important, they appear on many Chinese objects and buildings, because the owners of these objects and buildings were asking the dragons to look kindly on both themselves and their families and descendants.

A mandarin's embroidered silk robe from the Ch'ing dynasty (1796-1820)

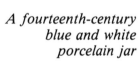

A fourteenth-century blue and white porcelain jar

Part of the Screen of the Nine Dragons in the Inner Court of the Imperial Winter Palace, Peking

The Lost Secret

by Joan Cameron
illustrated by June Jackson

Far across the China Seas, in a hidden land of mountains and rivers, ruled the Grand Mandarin of Hai Fu. He was an old man, with a long black pigtail and a thin black moustache which drooped down to his knees. His almond-shaped eyes looked so calmly over the world that his people almost never knew what he was thinking. To be safe, they always tried to please him. They knew only too well that if they did not, the Imperial Headchopper-in-Chief would be busy sharpening his two-handed sword.

Every afternoon the Grand Mandarin sat on the sun terrace with his Imperial peacocks. At three o'clock on the dot, he took tea, sipping the golden liquid, piping hot, from a fragile china cup.

Except for today. He sat, and the sun moved across the sky. And the Imperial Tea did not come. The peacocks moved restlessly. Even they knew that something had GONE WRONG.

The Grand Mandarin tapped his long fingers on the arm of his chair, the only sign of anger he ever gave. The shadows had moved across the grass, and the sun no longer shone on the tinkling fountains. Tea time was long past.

The Chief of the Imperial Household came nervously on to the terrace.

'I am waiting.' The Grand Mandarin's voice was thin. 'I am waiting for the Imperial Tea.'

The Chief of the Imperial Household bowed so low that his black hair almost touched the ground. 'We have had an accident,' he tried to explain.

'An accident?'

'Yes, your Imperial Majesty,' said the Chief of the Imperial Household. 'We have had an accident in the Royal Kitchens. But your tea is here now.' He clapped his hands and servants in gold uniforms brought in the Imperial Tea Tray. They set it on the table by the Grand Mandarin's chair, and stood back. The Chief of the Imperial Household poured pale golden tea into his master's cup.

With a sigh of relief, the Grand Mandarin lifted the cup between long fingers, and took a sip. Then he dashed the cup to the ground, where it smashed into a thousand pieces. The Grand Mandarin raised his arms in fury and shook his fist at the Chief of the Imperial Household.

'My tea is COLD!' he roared.

The peacocks fluttered away in panic. Never before had the Grand Mandarin been heard to shout in such rage! He turned to the Chief of the Imperial Household.

'Well?' he demanded. 'Explain! Why is the Imperial cup of tea cold?'

The Chief of the Imperial Household bowed so low he was almost on his hands and knees.

'We – we had an accident in the Imperial Kitchens, your Imperial Majesty,' he stammered. 'We – we lost something...'

'You LOST something?'

'Well, perhaps I should say we mislaid something. Something rather important.'

The Grand Mandarin threw the cold teapot right across the terrace, just missing one of his peacocks.

'Explain!' he roared, his patience gone.

'We lost – we mislaid –'

'Yes?'

'We have mislaid the secret of fire.' The Chief of the Imperial Household hung his head.

There was a terrible silence. The Grand Mandarin's brows drew down into a dreadful frown.

'How can this be?'

'We don't know, your Imperial Majesty,' said the Chief of the Imperial Household, unhappily. 'We've looked everywhere, but the Imperial Kitchen fires are all out. Every single one. And no one knows how to light them again.'

'No one at all?'

'No, your Imperial Majesty,' said the Chief of the Royal Household. Then, greatly daring: 'Perhaps you —'

'No!' The Grand Mandarin shouted. 'Our Imperial Majesty does not know! Find someone who does!' And he stalked off the terrace in a rage.

The Chief of the Royal Household issued a proclamation. By next morning it was known all over Hai Fu that the secret of fire had been lost in the palace. No one could help. Every fire in the whole of Hai Fu was a cold pile of white ash, and not a soul knew how to light them. The Grand Mandarin was so miserable that he even forgot to send for the Imperial Headchopper-in-Chief.

Days went past, and the Grand Mandarin grew more unhappy by the minute. The Imperial Kitchens tried everything to tempt him, from grape juice to goat's milk and honey, but he sent it all back, barely tasted.

From beneath a weeping willow in the Imperial Gardens, a little gardener's boy called Lee Ping watched his Grand Mandarin's unhappiness.

'I would like to help our Imperial Majesty,' he told the Imperial Chief Gardener one night as they ate their cold supper.

'You? How can a small boy help when all the Palace can't?'

Lee Ping stared down into his empty supper bowl. What he saw there gave him a wonderful idea! He rushed across the garden to the Imperial Library, and there, on the wall, he found a map of Hai Fu. He'd seen it there while filling the Imperial flower vases.

He followed the River Hai with his finger. The river led to the Hai Fu mountains, and the Caves of Ice. Under that spot someone had written something: 'Here be —'

When he saw what the third word was, Lee Ping danced a little jig. He folded the map, put it in his pocket, and off he went.

More than a week passed. The Palace people missed the little gardener's boy, and some even said he was dead. But he wasn't. It was a long way to the Hai Fu mountains and the Caves of Ice. And he was only a very little gardener's boy, after all.

He came back one afternoon, tired, dirty, but very happy. Draped round his shoulders was a very odd-looking silver lizard. Or was it a lizard? No one had ever seen such a creature. Except in pictures, or painted on china, or maybe on very old maps.

Lee Ping marched on to the Imperial terrace, uninvited. 'Here is the secret of fire, your Imperial Majesty,' he said proudly. 'He's only a little one, but the others wouldn't come with me.'

Mouth open in astonishment, the Grand Mandarin stared at the little creature. It opened its mouth, and out shot what was unmistakably a little burst of flame. The secret of fire was back in the Palace, thanks to a little gardener's boy — and an even smaller dragon!

That afternoon, the Grand Mandarin sat on the terrace and took tea, piping hot once again. He had an important guest — a very sleepy gardener's boy. The Grand Mandarin sipped his tea. It was just as he liked it.

'How did you come to think of dragons?' he said at last. 'No one else did, not even me.'

'They were painted all over my supper bowl,' Lee Ping answered simply. 'And I'd seen this.'

He pulled the map out of his pocket, smoothed out the creases, and held it out to the Grand Mandarin. Under the Caves of Ice someone had written words that are often seen on ancient maps: 'Here be dragons.'

'I wrote that myself,' said His Imperial Majesty humbly. 'But I didn't remember about the dragons. Neither did anyone else. But you did. One day, when you're a little bigger, you will be Chief of the Imperial Household.'

But the little gardener's boy didn't hear him. He'd fallen asleep amongst the teacups.

And the dragon? He liked the Palace so much that he stayed, and became the Imperial China Tea Dragon. And no one in Hai Fu ever again lost the secret of fire.

33

Sam's Secret

by Mary Hurt

illustrated by Anne Close

When Sam's Mummy came back from town one Saturday he was glad to see her. He was feeling a bit fed up because it had been raining all morning and Daddy had been too busy doing jobs around the house to play with him. So when Mummy arrived home with two bags of shopping and asked him to help her to unpack everything he was glad to have something to do at last.

Carefully he lifted the packages out of the bags. First biscuits, then tea, orange juice, sugar – he knew where to put them all in the cupboards. Mummy wouldn't let him take the eggs out of their boxes as they were too fragile. But as she was unpacking them she called to Sam, 'My goodness! What a big egg this is. Just look. I don't think I've ever seen one as big as this.'

Sam looked into the box of eggs, and saw that one of them was a lot bigger than the others. Mummy put it on top of the others in a basket where she always kept the eggs. Then she put the basket on the worktop, saying, 'I bet you'll enjoy that one for your breakfast tomorrow. Perhaps there will even be two yolks in it.'

Sam had never seen an egg with two yolks before, so he was looking forward to that. But that egg did not end up on Sam's plate next morning, as you will see.

That night Sam went to bed at seven o'clock as usual. But he woke up suddenly in the middle of the night. The moonlight was shining through his window.

Sam climbed out of bed and tiptoed downstairs to the kitchen. He stood very still, and in the silence he could hear a crackling noise. He listened again, and realised that the sound was coming from the basket of eggs on the worktop.

In the light from the windows he could see that the largest egg was slowly cracking open. Then suddenly it rolled out of the basket and on to the worktop, breaking open completely. Sam stared as a strange little creature appeared from out of the broken egg. It was a curious and bedraggled looking animal which Sam did not recognise at first. But after it had shaken out its wings and stretched itself, Sam was amazed to see that it looked very much like a dragon in one of his story books, although this one was a lot smaller, of course. Sam stared and stared. He couldn't really believe what he was seeing.

Then the loveliest thing happened. The tiny creature, who had been too busy stretching itself to notice Sam, suddenly looked straight at him. Then he gave a big wink and smiled a great big smile. Sam could not help but smile back and from that moment on he knew they were going to be the best of friends.

The next minute, the dragon fluttered down on to the floor and as Sam watched in astonishment, it grew bigger and bigger. They went out into the garden together, and outside in the moonlight Sam was able to see that the dragon was a rather beautiful creature with scaly skin which shimmered like rich, dark green silk.

Sam climbed on to the dragon's back and held on tightly around the creature's neck. The dragon spread its magnificent wings and away they flew into the night sky.

Soon Sam could see the tree tops and street lights disappearing far below him. Then they were left far behind as they soared on into the darkness. Sam knew they must be going to a magic, far away place.

It wasn't long before he saw a light shining in the distance. They seemed to be flying towards it. Then they touched the ground and Sam saw that the light was coming from the entrance to an enormous cave. He climbed down from the dragon's back and followed him towards the cave.

When he got to the entrance of the cave Sam saw a most beautiful sight. The cave was lit by a thousand candles and coloured jewels sparkled on the walls. It was the most wonderful, magical place Sam had ever seen and the cave was full of dragons of all shapes and sizes; their lovely green scales shimmering in the candlelight.

The little dragon whispered to Sam that this was the big dragon party which was only held every hundred years and every dragon was invited to it.

As soon as Sam and the dragon went into the cave all the dragons cheered and roared a great welcome. Then the party began. They all danced and sang and played games. And the dancing got faster and the singing louder on and on into the night. Sam thought it was the best party he'd ever been to but he was beginning to feel tired.

He went to sit down at the side of the cave and watched as the dragons carried on dancing.

He didn't want to close his eyes; he didn't want to miss one moment of the party, but his eyelids were closing and his head nodding. Soon Sam was fast asleep with sounds of the happy dragons still ringing in his ears.

Someone was calling his name. 'Sam... Sam... You *are* a sleepy head this morning. Wake up. There's a good boy.'

Slowly Sam opened his eyes. Where was he? He was not in the cave of dragons. Can you guess where he was? Yes! He was in his own bed at home, and Mummy was trying to wake him up. When she saw that he was awake, she left him, saying, 'Hurry up. Don't forget. You've got that lovely big egg for breakfast today.'

The egg! What had happened to it? Sam leapt out of bed and ran downstairs at top speed. Into the kitchen he flew.

'Mummy...' he began, but Mummy and Daddy had already discovered the broken egg and were both looking at it in amazement.

'Well, I never!' said Daddy. 'Whatever has happened to this?'

Sam smiled a secret smile. It would be his very own special secret for always.

Elmer

by Pat Baker

illustrated by Gillian Hurry

Elmer was a very young dragon. He was only two hundred and fifty three years old. He was always asking questions, because he wanted to know all about *everything*. His favourite word was, 'Why?'

Elmer's mother, Eloise, was always much too busy to answer his questions. Every day, she had to clean the cave where they lived, and after that, she had to go out to collect the things that dragons like to eat. Back she would come, carrying fresh tree roots and juicy fruits. When she wasn't cleaning or finding food, she spent her time scorching beautiful fiery pictures on to the walls of the cave.

So when Elmer asked Eloise, 'Why this?' or 'Why that?' she would look down at him absentmindedly, puff pale blue smoke and say softly, 'Go and ask your father, dear.'

Elmer's father, Eustace, was quite different. Eloise sometimes called him Useless Eustace, which was really rather naughty of her! Eustace, I'm afraid, was a very lazy dragon. He spent his time dozing in the sun or practising his deep fire breathing, when he wasn't eating delicious snacks or drinking from the deep green waters of the pool near the cave.

When Elmer asked Eustace, 'Why this?' or 'Why that?', he would yawn a cloud of hazy, grey smoke and say slowly, 'Er – I can't remember, son.' Poor Elmer! How was he to learn if no one would answer his questions?

Elmer's favourite place was down on the beach. He would wander as far as the second cave in the high cliff and no further. This was because his mother had told him once that he was never to go past that cave, though she hadn't told him why.

One sunny morning, Elmer asked again why he could not go further. His mother told him to ask his father. His father yawned and puffed grey smoke, and paid no attention. Elmer waited a little while to see if his father was going to tell him. Then he thought that if he went a little further, he might find out why for himself.

So off he went past the first cave, over the black rocks covered in slippery green seaweed, and on past the second cave – feeling very excited but a little guilty. Suddenly, in the distance, Elmer saw something strange. Two small animals, walking on their hind legs, were splashing in the sea. Elmer thought it looked great fun, and decided to go and join them.

36

He galloped happily along the beach towards them, then the smile dropped from his face, and he stopped dead in his tracks. The two small animals were running away; they were frightened! Elmer turned away and walked sadly back along the beach.

When Elmer reached the cave, he found his mother busy digging and his father dozing in the sun. Elmer didn't bother to ask them about the two strange animals and why they had run away. They wouldn't answer anyway. He gave an impatient puff of yellow smoke, and he decided to go back after lunch and see if he could find out for himself.

When he had eaten, Elmer felt much more cheerful and full of hope. Along the beach he strode. He was so excited that small puffs of bright red smoke came from his nostrils.

He went quite a long way along the beach before he found more of the same strange animals. This time there were seven of them. Three were splashing in the shallow water on the edge of the sea, and four were playing on the sand with what looked like a very colourful moon. As he came nearer, Elmer thought of calling out to them, but just as he opened his mouth one of the small animals gave a frightened shout. He pointed towards Elmer, and suddenly they were all shouting and running away from him.

At first Elmer started to run after them, but they ran so fast that he could not keep up. He flopped down on to the sand and sobbed loud dragon sobs. Then through his sobs, Elmer heard a very small voice. 'What's the matter, dragon?' it said.

Elmer looked up and through his tears he saw one of the strange animals. It was kneeling beside him and its body was yellow at the top and red at the bottom.

Elmer sobbed unhappily, 'I saw some animals like you, playing. It looked such fun that I wanted to play too, but when they saw me they ran away. Please – please do you know why?'

At this the small boy – for a boy it was – looked almost as sad as Elmer. 'I don't know,' said the boy, and then he explained. His father, Michael, was always very busy. He spent his time wallpapering and painting. When the house was smart and clean he would go out shopping at the large supermarket to buy things that boys liked to eat. Back he would come with tins of baked beans and packets of crisps. When he wasn't decorating the house or shopping, he would be busy digging the garden, or making things with wood.

The boy's mother, Maisie, was quite different. Michael sometimes called her Lazy Maisie, which was really rather naughty of him. Maisie, I'm afraid, was a very idle lady. She hardly ever did any work, and she spent a lot of her time just lying in the sun. When she wasn't sunbathing she sat eating chocolates, or sipping lemonade through a long coloured straw.

'When I ask 'Why?' said the boy, 'Dad hasn't time and Mum can't remember.'

Elmer grinned widely. 'I'm Elmer,' he said. 'My Mum and Dad are like that too.' And he told the boy about Eloise and Eustace, and how they never answered his questions.

'I'm Martin,' said the boy. 'Shall we be friends?' Neither of them needed to ask why!

From then on, Elmer met Martin by the second cave in the high cliff every day. They would play together in the sea, and then they would talk together – and between them, they found the answers to a great many questions!

Spiky the Sea Dragon

by Joan Cameron

illustrated by Keith Logan

One stormy day the Sea Witch flew low over the North Sea. The wind blew hard, and she had to crouch over her broomstick. Under her cloak she clutched a basket of dragons' eggs, a gift for the Welsh Dragon King from the Trolls of Norway.

An extra hard gust of wind almost snatched her black hat clean away. She let go of the basket for a second, to push the hat back on to her seaweedy hair. Before she could steady it once more, the basket wobbled, and unknown to her, one dragon's egg fell out.

It landed with a splash in the sea, and sank slowly, to settle in a clump of seaweed. There it lay, until one bright morning, a crack appeared in its shell. The crack grew wider and wider, until the egg split open. Out popped a little green dragon.

He looked around once or twice, and nodded happily to himself. If he wondered where all the other dragons were, he said nothing. He gave all his attention to settling into his new home.

That is how Spiky, the Sea Dragon, came to live in the North Sea. He grew up with only the wind and waves for company. He kept himself to himself.

Spiky loved the wild North Sea. There were no other dragons about, so it was all his own. He liked it best when it was rough. Then he would play across the huge waves. With great roars and puffs of smoke, he would leap through the spray. The smoke was often steam, for the bigger waves nearly put his fire out!

Ships sometimes came near. When they did, Spiky sank under the waves. There he would wait, his fire damped down, until they passed. Fish sometimes came upon him. Most darted away in fright, for Spiky was a fearsome sight. But he would not have harmed any of them. He was the shyest dragon who ever lived.

Years passed, happy years of huffing and puffing, and keeping himself to himself. He grew older. His fire turned from red to deep orange, and his scales turned a deeper green. He still played his games with the North Sea waves, but only the smaller ones. To tell the truth, when the sea water put his fire out, it wasn't so easy to start it up again. It was safer to sink below the waves until the sea was calm again.

The North Sea grew busier. Spiky found himself hiding from ships more often. Odd, stubby little ships they were, with twin funnels and long, low sterns.

One day a strange structure appeared. It stood on huge legs, and didn't look like a ship at all. Indeed, it needed tugs to pull it through the water. Spiky had never seen anything like it. To his horror, it stopped, and big anchors were laid on the bottom of the sea to keep it in place.

'What can it be?' he gasped.

That night Spiky crept through the dark waves. Keeping his fire down so that no one would see, he floated quietly in the water. He watched, and listened. That night he heard new words: 'North Sea Oil', 'Oil Rig', and 'Oilfield.' What were they? What was happening?

Sadly, Spiky made up his mind. He would have to look for somewhere else to live. But where? He hoped the Sea Witch would pay him a visit so that he could ask her. But she didn't come. More ships came instead, and helicopters whirred overhead. It was time to leave.

Early one morning, Spiky said goodbye to his favourite patch of sea. He turned west. He swam and swam, and rested when he was tired. Now and then he huffed and puffed, for practice. Every so often he had to sink down under the waves, as ships and fishing boats crossed his path. At length the coast came into sight.

Spiky stopped suddenly. He had never seen land before. He was so surprised that he let his fire go out. Once he had got it going again, he swam towards the cliffs, keeping low in the water.

That oil rig was only the first of many. Now the North Sea was busy. More oil rigs came, and more ships. Sometimes blobs of thick black liquid floated on top of the sea. Spiky hated it. It clogged his scales and got into his eyes.

A rocky cliff loomed above him. Spiky stared. What was this? As he wondered, a fleet of fishing boats sailed out from a little harbour not far away. He sank down, out of their way.

Down he went. The sea was shallow here, and soon his claws touched the sandy bottom. The cliff face rose straight up out of the water, like a wall.

Halfway along, he suddenly saw a tunnel entrance, near the foot of the cliff. Curiously, he darted into it, steering with his tail. Inside, it was dark, but he swam bravely on and on until he was quite tired. A faint glow appeared ahead, and all at once, the tunnel ended. Spiky swam into brightness.

He found himself in another sea. At least he thought it was, but the water didn't feel the same. It didn't taste the same either. There was no salt in it.

Cautiously, Spiky swam up to the surface. If this was another sea, it was a very small one, with land all around it. It seemed to be quiet, too. Spiky decided to stay.

The sun shone brightly. Spiky floated on his back, giving a little huff of contentment. He was tired after his long journey. Soon he drifted off to sleep.

42

He hadn't been asleep for long when a deep voice woke him up. 'Who are you?'

Spiky opened his eyes. He found himself face to face with the biggest surprise of his life. A big head, at the end of a long neck, reared up out of the water beside him. Two big eyes looked into his.

'I'm not the only one after all!' cried Spiky. 'You're another Sea Dragon!'

'No, no, laddie!' chuckled the other. 'I'm not exactly a dragon. I'm quite friendly, really. Where did you come from?'

Spiky gave a damp puff. 'I used to live in the North Sea,' he said sadly. 'But it's so

Spiky looked at him. True enough, he wasn't *quite* a dragon. He didn't have any scales, and he couldn't huff and puff. His body was much bigger. But what did these things matter? 'I'll stay,' he said.

As they swam along together, Spiky asked: 'What is this sea called?'

His new friend grinned. 'Didn't you know, laddie?' he cried. 'This isn't a sea. This is Loch Ness.'

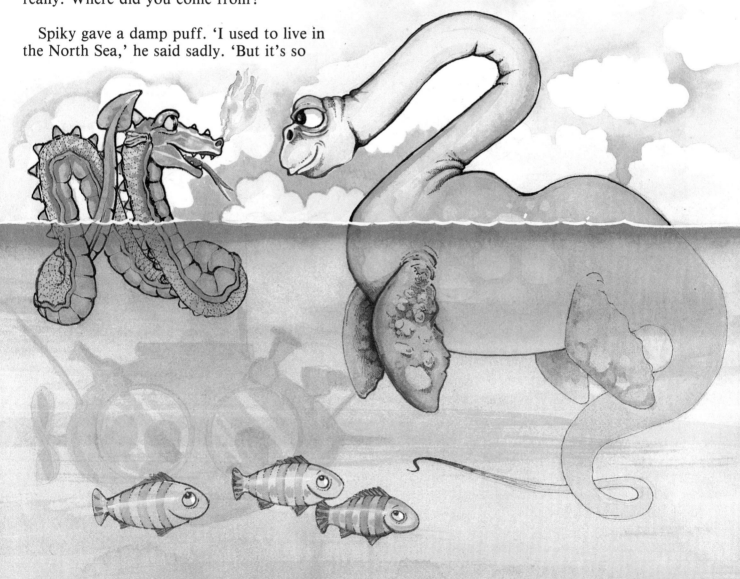

busy now, I had to leave. I came here through a tunnel.'

It was the other's turn to look sad.

'I can't get through that tunnel,' he said. 'My body's too big. I have to stay here. I've been so lonely, because everyone runs away from me. Will you stay? Please?'

'I think I'll like it here,' laughed Spiky.

And he gave a big puff of orange flame in sheer excitement.

Everyone has heard of the Loch Ness Monster. But keep this story to yourself – not everyone knows that there are *two* monsters there now!

Willie the Water Dragon

by Charlie Chester

illustrated by Drury Lane Studios

A long time ago in a place called Dragonia, there was great excitement, for a very special new baby dragon was born.

The father of this new baby dragon was the biggest and strongest of all the dragons. He could breathe more fire, and blow more smoke, than any other dragon, and when the baby was born, he was so excited he offered to give a fiery display of his great talents.

'Let it be known,' he said, 'that I intend to blow a sheet of flame at least ten feet long! I shall stand that distance from a tree and set it alight,' he went on boastfully. 'After that, I shall take some deep breaths and then send up a cloud of smoke that will darken the heavens for at least three miles around!'

'Can you really do that?' asked the other dragons.

'Oh yes, you'll be surprised at what I can do,' he replied, and off he went to practise the great feats he intended to display.

Meanwhile, the other dragons were busy building a Grand Palace which was to be in the centre of the great square in Dragonia.

While all this activity was going on, the new baby's mother noticed something unusual...for happy though it seemed to be, the baby dragon wasn't breathing smoke at all, and not a sign of any fire came from its mouth. Instead, it simply squirted water!

'I just don't understand it at all,' she said. 'He's not a bit like any ordinary dragon. All he does is gurgle and squirt water; it's most upsetting.' Months went by, and still the little dragon only squirted water. So the doctor was sent for.

'There's nothing wrong with him,' the doctor said, after testing the baby thoroughly. 'He's got a fine head, a powerful body, his claws are strong and he's got a magnificent tail. Perhaps he'll grow out of it later when he's a bit older.'

'I certainly hope so,' the mother replied. 'After all, who wants a dragon that can't breathe smoke and fire; it's just not natural. All the other dragon children will laugh at him.' So saying, she tucked the baby up in his cot, and opened the window so that the water he kept squirting could go out of the house and across the field.

45

As time went by, the baby got bigger and bigger, but there was still no sign of any smoke or fire from his large mouth. None of the other children wanted to play with him, and he became very unhappy.

'Are you still going to give your fire display?' his mother asked her husband.

'Well, I suppose I shall have to, now,' said his father. 'After all, I did tell everyone that I would. If I don't give a display, they'll think I just can't do all the things I said I would, and I have been practising some very startling feats.'

After many more weeks of work and practice the Grand Palace was finished. On the date set for the great display, the dragons met in the huge village square. For safety, all the children were taken into the Grand Palace and allowed to look out of the windows.

There was great excitement everywhere. When King Dragon, as he was known, took a deep breath and blew a cloud of smoke twenty feet long, they all clapped like mad. His next feat was to stand fifteen feet away from some tree logs and after huffing and puffing, he sent out of his mouth a flame so long, it set fire to the logs.

Everybody cheered and waggled their enormous tails.

Then King Dragon started to cough because of the extra black smoke coming from his nostrils. Although he couldn't stop coughing, everyone thought it was part of the act and laughed and cheered once more.

King Dragon, however, didn't see the funny side of it as he rolled on his back and coughed and coughed. Each time he coughed flames and sparks and smoke poured from him, much to the delight and admiration of the crowd.

Suddenly there was a gasp, as with a bellowing roar King Dragon gave a really huge cough, and a sheet of flame shot from him towards the Palace.

In seconds the palace was on fire – and all the children were inside.

There was panic. Mothers began to scream and fathers looked on in dismay. The children were shouting from the windows, as smoke and fire surrounded them.

'What are we going to do?' someone cried.

'What *can* we do?' someone else answered.

Then, suddenly, from out of the crowd stepped the little baby dragon. He stood at least twenty feet from the flaming palace and he began gurgling. His mouth opened, and instead of fire and smoke a stream of water came out, just like a fireman's hose. As he coughed and squirted, he drenched the palace with water, and the fire was quickly put out.

All the children were rescued, and the parents were so grateful that the baby dragon was given a special party. They even made him a present of the Grand Palace, and he lives there to this very day.

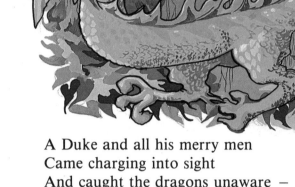

The Plight of
the Rainbow Dragons

by June Woodman and Rita Grainge

illustrated by Kathie Layfield

In ancient woods of Dragon Land
Not far as dragons fly,
Despair and sadness filled all hearts
And here's the reason why.

There were no baby dragons left
To carry on the race —
The dragon line was dying out
And sad was every face.

No ordinary dragons these,
But ones with special powers;
They changed their colours as they sat
On grass, or trees, or flowers.

Then one fine day, the joyful news
Spread round for miles and miles —
Their Queen had laid a giant egg,
And sadness turned to smiles.

The smiles soon grew to laughter as
They danced, and pranced with glee.
They put their favourite colours on
And cheered wholeheartedly!

A competition then was held
To see who looked the best.
The Rainbow Queen was asked to judge
And climbed down from her nest.

But while she gazed at stripes and dots
And patterns round and square,
The sound of hunting horns rang out
And barking filled the air.

A Duke and all his merry men
Came charging into sight
And caught the dragons unaware —
There was no time for flight.

The only thing that they could do
Was use their special powers.
They quickly lost their stripes and spots
And merged with trees and flowers.

"There's nothing here," the Duke declared.
"The hunting's poor today."
"I beg to differ," smiled one knight,
And snatched the egg away!

"I've never seen an egg so big!"
The knight was heard to boast.
"And after jousting day we'll all
Have scrambled egg on toast!"

48

In great high glee they rode away
With laughter and with cheers.
The Rainbow Dragons wept and wailed,
Their Queen shed rainbow tears.

The Rainbow Queen was furious.
"We'll thwart their wicked plan.
No scurvy knave shall put OUR egg
Into a frying-pan!"

They drew up in formation and
Into the sky they flew —
But nobody could see them for
They'd changed to white and blue.

Arriving at the Palace, they
All landed in the yard,
Then played a game of hide-and-seek
To dodge the Palace Guard.

They scattered left and right to search
In every likely place,
And some unlikely places too —
The search went on a-pace.

One looked into the kitchen, but
The egg was not in sight,
And when the cook
        came through the door
He changed to flour-white.

One crept into the bedroom, where
He searched and searched in vain,
But no one saw him, for he matched
The Royal counterpane.

They used their special powers for
searching high and low,
All blending with the furnishings
Wherever they did go.

But NOWHERE could they find their egg,
Though searching frantically,
Until the Rainbow Queen announced,
"I know where it will be!"

Without another word she crept
Into the Room of Thrones,
And found the egg in pride of place
Among the precious stones.

Then stealthily and silently
They stole their egg away,
And back to Dragon Land they flew —
Their powers had saved the day.

Can you imagine all the fuss,
And cries, and sobs, and scenes?
"We've lost the egg!" "There'll be no feast!"
"We'll have to eat baked beans!"

Can you imagine the DELIGHT
And joy in Dragon Land?
"We've FOUND our egg! We'll have a feast!"
The queen gave her command.

They put their favourite colours on
And danced and pranced with glee.
Then, suddenly the egg cracked wide,
And there for all to see

Two baby dragons, boy and girl,
Were gurgling happily.
Now Dragon Land was safe, with such
A Rainbow Nursery!

The Lazy Brothers

by Mary Hurt

illustrated by Robert Ayton

Long ago in a faraway land, there lived two brothers, Ivan and Sergio. They were a lazy pair who liked to lie around the house all day doing nothing at all.

One evening after supper their father suddenly became very angry with them. He yelled, 'You leave this house tomorrow! It's time you looked after yourselves. I've had enough of your idle ways.'

So next day the two brothers packed their belongings and sadly left home, wondering what on earth was to become of them. But their father was glad to see them go!

The two brothers strolled along the country lanes in the sunshine for a while and soon became hungry, for their father had sent them away without any breakfast.

Presently they noticed a field of golden corn ready to be harvested. They were so hungry that Ivan said to his brother, 'Perhaps if we cut the corn, the owner of the field will pay us for the work. Then we'll be able to buy food.'

So they set to work at once, but it took a very long time. They had never worked before in their lives, so they just weren't used to it.

When late in the day they stopped for a rest, they heard a heavy rumbling noise above their heads. They looked up, and were horrified to see an ugly black dragon sitting in a nearby tree.

'Good afternoon. What are you doing here?' asked the dragon, with a sly smile.

'W-well,' stammered Ivan, 'we were hoping that the owner of this field might pay us for cutting his corn. We've eaten nothing all day and we're very hungry.'

'Oh, are you?' replied the dragon, curling and uncurling his long tail around the trunk of the tree. 'Then today is your lucky day. I own this field, and if you will take a letter to my wife, she will give you a good dinner in return for your work.'

As he was speaking, he quickly wrote a letter. He closed the envelope so that the brothers could not read it.

But Ivan and Sergio did not trust the dragon. So when they had gone a little way they opened up the envelope and were shocked to read this!

Dear Mrs Dragon,

Please cook these two boys for my supper. Don't forget to put in plenty of salt and pepper.

Love, Mr Dragon.

The two brothers thought for a while, then they tore up the letter and wrote another. It said,

Dear Mrs Dragon,

These two boys have very kindly cut our field of corn. Please give them a hearty dinner and send them on their way with plenty of food for their journey, and our fastest horse to speed them along.

Love,
Mr Dragon.

'If you are so clever,' he said with a smile, 'perhaps you can do something for me. Many years ago the dragon stole a beautiful bedspread from my palace. This cover is encrusted with precious jewels and I would dearly love to have it back. Many brave young men have tried to get it, but the dragon has eaten every one of them. If you could bring it back to me, I would reward you with great riches.'

When they arrived at the dragon's home they showed the letter to Mrs Dragon. She made them very welcome and gave them a delicious meal of roast beef, roast potatoes, carrots and turnips, followed by plum pudding, which was their favourite. After dinner, while they had a rest, Mrs Dragon saddled a fine black horse and prepared two huge baskets full of bread, cheese, fruit and wine for their journey.

The boys continued on their way, laughing at the crafty way they had tricked the dragon. In fact, they talked about it so much that the king soon got to hear of it, and sent for them in order that they might tell him their story.

The idea of great riches pleased the brothers, for then they would never have to work again. For many days they pondered, searching for a plan to trick the dragon once more.

Then one day as they sat in the sun, thinking hard, Ivan suddenly jumped up, shouting, 'I've got it! I've thought of a plan!' He had been watching some ants which were scurrying around nearby, and he had remembered that dragons were frightened of ants. He found the ants' nest, and filled a bag with them, tying it tightly so that they could not get out.

That night he and his brother set off in the darkness for the dragon's house. When they reached it, they crept quickly up to the bedroom window and peered inside. There lay Mr and Mrs Dragon, sleeping peacefully, their long tails coiled round the bedposts. On top of them lay the beautiful cover, glinting with hundreds of jewels in the moonlight.

Silently the two brothers climbed through the open window, emptied the ants on the bedspread, and tiptoed out again.

Presently Mr Dragon's nose began to twitch as several ants marched across it. 'What's that?' he muttered drowsily, flicking the end of his long tail across his nose. But as the tickling got worse he rubbed his eyes and opened them. Thousands of ants were marching across the bedspread — not to mention his face!

With a terrified yell, he leapt out of bed. He dragged the cover off and hurled it through the open window, ants and all! Mrs Dragon snored on. She had not noticed anything at all!

Outside in the darkness, Ivan and Sergio could hardly believe their luck when the bedspread came flying out of the window, just as they had hoped it would.

They were so busy laughing and dancing that they forgot all about the dragon. But he had quickly shaken the ants from his face and, wondering what the noise was about, peered out into the moonlight where Ivan and Sergio were screaming with laughter.

When he realised that he had once more been tricked by the two brothers, he fell into a rage. Fire bellowed from his mouth, and with a terrifying roar of anger he leapt through the window, spread his mighty wings and in seconds he was upon them.

The brothers, too frightened to move, were gobbled up in seconds.

'A tasty supper,' said the dragon out loud. 'And all the tastier for waiting!' And, picking up the bedspread, he went back inside. He climbed into bed beside his still snoring wife, pulled the cover into place and fell fast asleep.

Picking it up, they laughed and danced for joy. Now, they thought, all their troubles would be over. They could live in idle luxury for the rest of their lives when the king paid them the gold which he had promised.

The next day was no better. This time it was not only Constable Coppit who was on the warpath, for every single garden fence in the whole of Bumblewick had been pushed over! All the villagers were furious, but still no one could find out who was playing these nasty tricks. Mr Grower was particularly cross because all his favourite flowers had been trampled on as well.

Then in the middle of Friday night, there was a most terrific crash, which awakened the whole village. It was ages before anyone felt brave enough to go and see what had happened, and then they found that all the pylons, right across the valley, had crashed to the ground! And by that time, there was nothing and no one to be seen.

This could not go on. Something had to be done! The villagers called a meeting, and decided that the men in the village should take turns to keep watch.

So the next night, when everyone else was asleep, several men stayed awake, watching and waiting. But that night, nothing happened. They watched every night for a week, and still nothing happened.

The villagers put their fences up again, men came to fix the pylons, and after that everything in Bumblewick was back to normal; peaceful and quiet.

Freddie the Clumsy Dragon

by L. M. Burden

illustrated by Hurlston Design Ltd

It all began one chilly Tuesday morning in the village of Bumblewick, a quiet little place where nothing ever seemed to happen.

It was so cold that nearly everyone was at home by the fire, snoozing. Then Constable Coppit, who was the only policeman for miles around, began to call at each house. He wanted to know if anyone knew what had happened to the trees in the park. Every single one had been knocked down, and completely flattened.

No one in the village knew anything about it at all, but they were very angry. They promised to tell Constable Coppit if they saw anything suspicious.

55

It was a long time before anyone knew what had caused the trouble, and it was a little girl called Emma who found out.

She was on her way home from school one day, taking the short cut through the woods, when she saw some enormous footprints in the snow. Emma stopped, terrified, then suddenly the creature who had made the footprints came into view, and she was no longer frightened.

It was a big green dragon with a long spiky tail and huge clumsy feet. His head hung down, and large tears rolled slowly down his scaly face and plopped into the snow.

Emma could not bear to see anyone crying, and she suddenly felt very sorry for him. So she looked up at him and asked, 'Can I help you?'

'No one can help me,' sobbed the dragon, whose name was Freddie. 'You see, I'm so clumsy. I can't see what I'm doing or where I'm going, and I'm always bumping into things and knocking them over. Look, I'm covered in bruises!' And he showed Emma some large purple bruises on his green scaly skin.

'Oh dear, it must have been you who knocked over all those things in our village,' said Emma. She thought hard for a moment, then she had a good idea. She took Freddie to see the wise old owl who lived high up in an oak tree nearby.

They woke him up and told him all about it. He stared hard at Freddie, then he said, 'Well, of course, if Freddie can't see, then he needs glasses! We should be able to do something about that.'

Emma and Freddie went back to see Owl a week later, and sure enough, when they arrived, he had found a great big pair of orange spectacles for Freddie.

The big dragon put them on, then blinked as he looked around. Slowly a big smile spread across his face. The whole world looked quite different! He could see the sunlight sparkling on the snow, and the scaly pattern of the bark on the oak tree – which was a bit like his own skin!

Freddie was so pleased that he danced for joy, without bumping into a single thing!

He thanked Owl, then he went with Emma into Bumblewick to say he was sorry for all the damage he had caused, and to tell them it would never happen again.

At first everyone looked crossly at him, but he began to work very hard doing odd jobs for all the villagers, and he became so useful that they soon forgave him.

As for Emma, he was so grateful to her for helping him that he gave her a ride on his back all the way to school every day, and waited for her outside the gates at hometime. Just imagine that!

The Chinese New Year Dragon

written and illustrated by Sheila Baker

The Imperial dragons were slightly different from the others – they had five claws on each foot instead of four.

Chinese people believed that dragons controlled the weather, and ceremonies were performed to please the dragons and gods in the hope of getting rain.

These ceremonies can still be seen today in all parts of the world. Children fly paper dragon kites high in the clouds, and during the Chinese New Year celebrations, large paper dragons are paraded through the streets with great festivity and fireworks.

The traditional head of a carnival dragon has large eyes and horns, an open mouth with long tongue and sharp teeth, and a flowing beard. Each head is decorated by the creators in their own way. The body may be either quite short, or may be a long length of brightly coloured scales and frills. The head is carried by one man, and the body is supported by dancing men as the dragon winds through the parade.

Unlike the wicked Western dragons, Chinese dragons were thought to bring good luck. There were five of them: heavenly dragons guarding the mansions of the gods; spiritual dragons taking care of the winds and the rain; earthly dragons controlling rivers, seas and floods; treasure dragons guarding treasure (very fierce); and Imperial dragons, the emblems of emperors.